hello, moon

Evan Turk

Atheneum Books for Young Readers
New York   London   Toronto   Sydney   New Delhi

Look! The Moon!
Should we go say hello?

hello, moon!

You look so beautiful tonight!
It's almost our bedtime,
but we'll see you again another night, Moon!

Don't worry, sweetheart, it's not gone. It's just hiding its face a little. Over the next two weeks, the Moon hides more and more until it looks like it disappears completely. We call that the New Moon.

It sounds like the Moon is feeling shy. Should we go out and say hello?

That's okay. Let's just walk together and enjoy the cold.

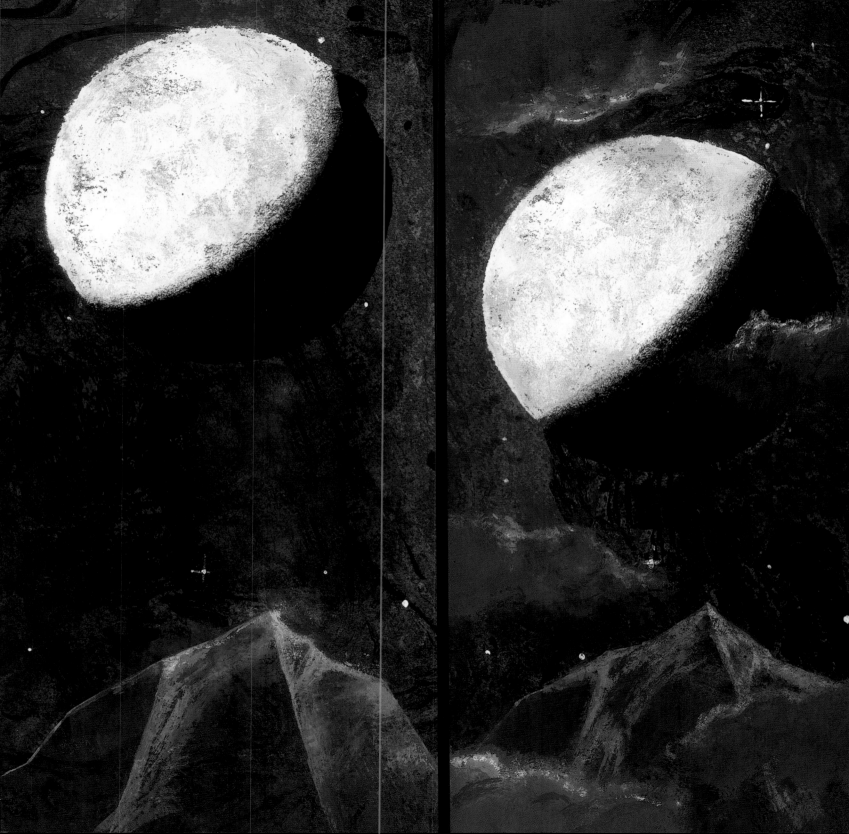

hello, moon!
We're almost being blown away tonight!
The wind and just half your light are enough
to make the forest feel alive!

hello, moon!
It's so quiet tonight.
Do you mind if we sit with you?
Sometimes all you need is someone
to share the silence with.

hello, moon!

It's such a crisp, clear night.
I can barely see you, but that's okay.

When we're together,
we don't have to be afraid of the dark.

Tonight is the night!
Let's go greet the New Moon!

hello, moon!

Are you there? It feels so dark.
You don't have to show your face tonight.
I know, not even the Moon feels like shining
all the time.

But look around, sweet Moon!

See how many stars are twinkling for you!
Sometimes when it seems dark, we get reminded
of how much light already surrounds us.

Don't worry, Moon.
We'll still be here,
    even when you're not shining.

And when you're ready,
  we'll gather
    all the stars together
      to welcome you back.

hello, moon!

To my nephew, Graham,
who I think of every time I look at the moon

A

ATHENEUM
BOOKS FOR YOUNG READERS
An imprint of Simon & Schuster Children's
Publishing Division • 1230 Avenue of the Americas,
New York, New York 10020 • © 2022 by Evan Turk •
Book design by Lissi Erwin and Sonia Chaghatzbanian
© 2022 by Simon & Schuster, Inc. • All rights reserved,
including the right of reproduction in whole or in part in any form. •
ATHENEUM BOOKS FOR YOUNG READERS is a registered trademark of
Simon & Schuster, Inc. • Atheneum logo is a trademark of Simon &
Schuster, Inc. • For information about special discounts for bulk purchases,
please contact Simon & Schuster Special Sales at 1-866-506-1949
or business@simonandschuster.com. • The Simon & Schuster Speakers Bureau
can bring authors to your live event. For more information or to book an event, contact the Simon & Schuster Speakers Bureau at 1-866-248-3049 or visit our website at
www.simonspeakers.com. • The text for this book was set in DanicaNovgorodoff. •
The illustrations for this book were made with marbling inks and gouache. •
Manufactured in China • 0522 SCP • First Edition • 10 9 8 7 6 5 4 3 2 1 • Library
of Congress Cataloging-in-Publication Data • Names: Turk, Evan, author, illustrator.
Title: Hello, Moon / Evan Turk. • Description: First edition. | New York :
Atheneum Books for Young Readers, [2022] | Audience: Ages 4 – 8. |
Summary: A parent and child explore the wonder of the changing moon
together. • Identifiers: LCCN 2021046643 | ISBN 9781534400801
(hardcover) | ISBN 9781534400818 (ebook) • Subjects:
CYAC: Moon—Fiction. | Mother and child—Fiction. | LCGFT:
Picture books. • Classification: LCC PZ7.1.T874 Hel
2022 | DDC [E]—dc23 LC record available at
https://lccn.loc.gov/2021046643